E
Bya

21669

Byars, Betsy

Hooray for the Golly
sisters!

copy #2

Hooray for the Golly Sisters!

Hooray for the Golly Sisters!

by
Betsy Byars

pictures by
Sue Truesdell

■ HarperCollins*Publishers*

I Can Read Book is a registered trademark of
HarperCollins Publishers.

Hooray for the Golly Sisters!
Text copyright © 1990 by Betsy Byars
Illustrations copyright © 1990 by Susan G. Truesdell
Printed in the U.S.A. All rights reserved.
Typography by Patricia Tobin
3 4 5 6 7 8 9 10

Library of Congress Cataloging-in-Publication Data
Byars, Betsy Cromer.
    Hooray for the Golly sisters! / by Betsy Byars ; pictures by Sue
Truesdell.
        p.   cm. — (An I can read book)
    Summary: In continued adventures, May-May and Rose take
their traveling road show to more audiences.
    ISBN 0-06-020898-8. — ISBN 0-06-020899-6 (lib. bdg.)
    [1. Sisters—Fiction.   2. Entertainers—Fiction.   3. Frontier and
pioneer life—Fiction.   4. West (U.S.)—Fiction.]   I. Truesdell,
Sue, ill.   II. Title.   III. Series.
PZ7.B9836Hm   1990   89-48147
[E]—dc20   CIP
                                                              AC

To Nina, with thanks

Table of Contents

The Golly Sisters Cross Big River

"Big river," said May-May.

"Very big river," said Rose.

"I think we should find another town,"

May-May said,

"a town on this side of the river."

Rose said, "No!

That town is waiting for us.

See the sign?"

WELCOME MAY-MAY

WELCOME ROSE

11

"Giddy-up!" said May-May.

The horse waded into the river.

He waded deeper into the river.

He began to swim in the river.

13

"We're floating away!" cried Rose.

"Good-bye, town," cried May-May.

"Good-bye, world," cried Rose.

14

"Iiiiiii!" yelled Rose.

"Eeeeeee!" yelled May-May.

May-May and Rose

closed their eyes.

THUMP.

May-May and Rose

opened their eyes.

The wagon was on shore.

"We're saved!" Rose cried.

"Look, May-May,

here is another town,

and another welcome sign."

WELCOME MAY-MAY

WELCOME ROSE

"We must be famous," said May-May.

"*Every* town knows us."

"Let's give a wonderful show,"

said Rose.

The Golly sisters headed for town.

Rose glanced over her shoulder.

"Big river," she said.

"Very big river," answered May-May.

May-May Does a Magic Act

"What are you doing

with those pigs?"

Rose asked.

"I am going to do my magic act,"

said May-May.

"May-May, why don't you

get some rabbits?"

"Everyone uses rabbits,"

said May-May.

"I want to be different."

That night Rose said,

"People!

For the first time on any stage,

May-May will make pigs disappear."

Behind the curtain May-May said,

"Pigs, don't let me down.

I will drop you into the hat.

You will slip

through a hole in the hat

and wait quietly

under the table."

May-May and the pigs went on stage.

"Ladies and gentlemen," she said,

"into my magic hat

I put one pig."

There was a soft thud

under the table.

24

"Into my magic hat

I put another pig."

There was another soft thud

under the table.

"I wave my wand.

Taaaaa-*daaaaa!*

The pigs have disappeared."

Suddenly a loud *Weeeeee*

came from under the table.

A boy said, "I hear the pigs.

The pigs are under the table."

Some people cried, "Boooooooo!"

May-May said,

"Now I will make the pigs reappear."

Before May-May could wave her wand,
the pigs ran out.

Now *everyone* cried, "Boooooooo!"

May-May said,

"I will make myself disappear too."

28

She walked off the stage.

29

Rose said, "Well, May-May,

at least we know one thing.

We know why magicians use rabbits."

"Yes," said May-May,

"rabbits don't go *Weeeeee*."

And that was the end

of the magic pigs.

The Golly Sisters Find a Swamp

"Well, we have done it now,"

said May-May.

"We are in a swamp."

31

"That is what I was afraid of,"
said Rose.

"And you know what lives in swamps,
don't you?" May-May asked.

"Yes, but don't say it," said Rose.

"I don't want to hear the word."

"I *have* to say it," said May-May.

"I want to make sure

we are thinking

about the same thing."

"What I am thinking about
is long and squiggly," said Rose.
May-May asked, "Is it a—"
"Don't say it!" said Rose.
"Please don't say it!"

"I can stop myself from *saying* it,"

May-May said,

"but I cannot stop myself

from *thinking* about it."

"I have an idea," said Rose.

"Let's take turns

thinking of nice things

that are in the swamp."

"Well, you and I are in the swamp,"

said May-May.

"We are nice."

"True, so true," said Rose.

"And the horse is in the swamp.

The horse is nice."

May-May said,

"I saw a bird back there.

I was about to say,

'Nice bird,' when . . . ."

"I see a beautiful flower," said Rose.

"And there is the sun,"

May-May said.

"And the blue sky!" said Rose.

"You know what

I have not thought about

in a long time?"

said May-May.

"What?" asked Rose.

"Can I go ahead and say it?

We are out of the swamp now."

"Go ahead," said Rose.

"Snake," said May-May.

"Snake!" said Rose.

"I was thinking crocodile."

"You were thinking crocodile?"

asked May-May.

"Yes," said Rose.

"Snake does not bother me.

See? Snake snake snake."

"Neither one bothers me,"

said May-May.

"Snake crocodile snake croc—

Oh, never mind," she said.

"Good-bye to both of them."

Rose Does the High-Wire Waltz

"Our show is blah," said Rose.

"I don't think so," said May-May.

"Our show is wonderful."

43

"Our show is blah," said Rose,

"but it will not be blah for long.

Tonight I will dance and sing

on the high wire."

May-May looked up.

"That high wire?" she asked.

"Yes," said Rose,

"and my song will be

'The High-Wire Waltz.'

I am going to practice now."

Rose climbed the tree.

She stepped on the high wire.

She sang:

Look at me

And you'll see

The high—wire—waltz!

The high wire began to shake.

Rose began to shake too.

She stopped singing.

May-May said, "What's wrong?"

Rose said, "I cannot move!"

May-May said, "Back up."

"I cannot back up," said Rose.

"I'm stuck!"

May-May said, "I will come get you."

May-May climbed the tree.

She took Rose's hand.

They climbed down the tree together.

Rose said sadly,

"Well, that is the end of that.

No high-wire waltz tonight."

"You could still do it,"

May-May said.

"How?" asked Rose.

"You could pretend to be
on the high wire," May-May said.
"You could draw a line,
like this."

"Oh, I like this so much better,"

said Rose,

"and I can still sing my song.

Look at me

And you'll see

The high—wire—waltz!

And the best thing!

No one will worry

that I might fall."

Hooray for the Golly Sisters!

"You know what I wish?" Rose said.

"What?" asked May-May.

"You will think this is silly,

but I wish someone would yell

'Hooray for the Golly Sisters!'

at the end of our show," said Rose.

"They clap," said May-May.

"Yes, they clap," said Rose,

"but I wish someone would yell

'Hooray for the Golly Sisters!'"

May-May said, "I wish that too."

May-May looked at Rose.

"Why are you smiling?"

asked May-May.

"When you smile like that,

I know you have an idea."

"Maybe," said Rose,

"but you are smiling too.

When you smile like that,

I know *you* have an idea."

"Maybe," said May-May.

57

That night after the show,

the people clapped.

The Golly Sisters took one bow.

58

Then Rose said, "Excuse me."

May-May said, "Excuse me."

The people kept clapping.

Suddenly

from one side

of the audience

came

"Hooray for

the Golly Sisters!"

Then

from the other side

came

"Hooray for

the Golly Sisters!"

The whole audience began to yell.

"Hooray for the Golly Sisters!

Hooray for the Golly Sisters!"

That night,

when the Golly sisters were in bed,

May-May said,

"You will think this is silly,

but I was the one who yelled,

'Hooray for the Golly Sisters!'"

Rose said,

"It is not silly at all.

I was the other one."

"It did sound good," said May-May.

"Wonderful!" said Rose.

With the hoorays

still ringing

in their heads,

the Golly sisters went to sleep.